The
FAITHFUL FRIEND

Robert D. San Souci · *illustrated by Brian Pinkney*

ALADDIN PAPERBACKS

First Aladdin Paperbacks edition January 1999
Text copyright © 1995 by Robert D. San Souci
Illustrations copyright © 1995 by Brian Pinkney
Aladdin Paperbacks
An imprint of Simon & Schuster Children's Publishing Division
1230 Avenue of the Americas
New York, NY 10020
Also available in a Simon & Schuster Books for Young Readers hardcover edition.
The text of this book was set in Packard
The illustrations were done in scratchboard and oil.
Manufactured in Mexico
20 19 18 17 16 15 14 13 12 11
The Library of Congress has cataloged the hardcover edition as follows:
San Souci, Robert D.
The faithful friend / Robert D. San Souci ; illustrated by Brian Pinkney—1st ed.
p.   cm.
Includes bibliographical references.
Summary: A retelling of the traditional tale from the French West Indies in which
two friends, Clement and Hippolyte, encounter love, zombies, and danger on the
island of Martinique.
[1. Folklore—Martinique.] I. Pinkney, J. Brian, ill. II. Title.
PZ8.1.S227Fai 1995
398.21—dc20 [E] 93-40672
ISBN 0-02-786131-7 (hc.)
ISBN 0-689-82458-0 (Aladdin pbk.)

GLOSSARY

(CAPITALS indicate stressed syllable)

Bon-Die (Bohn-DEHW): Good God; kind Lord

Bonjoú (BOH-zhew): Hello

Clement (CLEH-mahn): A man's name

Duforce (Due-FOR-seh): A family name

fer de lance (fair deh LON-seh): A poisonous snake (the name means literally, "fire-spear")

Hippolyte (EE-poh-leet): A man's name

Le Vauclin (Lay VOH-clan): A town in the southern portion of the island of Martinique

Macouba (Mah-COU-bah): A town at the northern end of the island of Martinique

Madinina (Ma-dee-NEE-na): "Island of Flowers"; original name for Martinique given by the Carib Indians

Martinique (Mar-tan-EEK): An island in the Caribbean where the people speak French with a "Creole" flavor

Missie (MIH-see): Mistress; madame; a polite form of address

Monfi' (MOHN-fee): My son; a form of address

Monsieur (MOHN-sur): Mister; sir; a polite form of address

Pauline (Pow-LINE): A woman's name

quimboiseur (kwim-BWAH-sur): A wizard

Zabocat (Zah-BOH-cah): A family name

To Dr. Arne Nixon,
a peerless educator, storyteller, and (best of all!) friend,
with thanks and affection
—R.S.S.

To my wife, Andrea,
and my friends Seth and Margie
—B.P.

IN THE LAST CENTURY, on the island of Martinique in the Caribbean Sea, there lived a man named Monsieur Duforce, who owned a sugar plantation. His wife had died giving birth to their only child, a boy named Clement. Monsieur Duforce hired a French-born widow, who lived in the nearby village of Le Vauclin, to be his son's nurse and tutor. She had given birth to her own son, Hippolyte, only a few days earlier. At Monsieur Duforce's insistence, Hippolyte was raised in the plantation house with Clement.

The boys grew into handsome young men—tall and lithe and sharp-witted. Clement's brown skin was the rich color of old bronze, while Hippolyte's fair skin was tanned by the tropic wind and sun. From the first they were as close as brothers.

One day, Clement showed his friend a small painting of a beautiful young woman. He said, "This is Pauline, the niece of Monsieur Zabocat, who lives at Macouba. I have fallen in love with her picture. Come with me tomorrow to visit her, so that I can ask her uncle for her hand in marriage."

At first, Hippolyte cautioned his friend, "A painting can tell only part of the story. You may arrive at Macouba to find she is sharp-tongued or dull-witted." Then he lowered his voice and added, "Some say that her uncle is a *quimboiseur*, a wizard. There may be danger in this adventure."

But when he saw that he could not change Clement's mind, he clasped his friend's hand and agreed to go. They were so close that the happiness of one was the happiness of both.

They set out the next day. Because the sun was hot, they walked slowly north along the coast road. Everywhere vivid blossoms blazed against the bright green of sugarcane and banana and pineapple fields and the deeper green of distant mountains. It was a perfect setting for the young men's high spirits.

But near Macouba, their joyful mood was broken when they discovered the body of an old beggar in the shade of a banana grove. They had passed by, when Hippolyte suddenly said, "It is wrong to ignore that poor man. We must go back and give him a proper burial."

Though Clement was eager to see Pauline, he agreed. At a nearby fishing village, they bought a simple coffin and arranged with the priest at the church to bury the unfortunate man in the little seaside cemetery.

In a quieter mood, they reached the vast plantation of Monsieur Zabocat, the uncle and guardian of Pauline.

"*Bonjou', Missie,* good day, sir," Clement said politely when he met the master of the house.

Monsieur Zabocat was a large man who stroked his thick mustache thoughtfully and offered Clement a guarded, "*Bonjou', Monfi',* good day, my son."

At that moment, Pauline hurried outside, eager to meet their guests. To both young men, she seemed cheerful as the morning sun. More beautiful than any painting, she was also lively and witty and clearly delighted to meet the two friends.

Clement, hopelessly in love, could only gaze at Pauline. Hippolyte talked of their journey (omitting only the sad incident of the beggar's funeral). All the time, he noticed the bright, loving smiles Pauline gave Clement and the dark looks Monsieur Zabocat cast on his friend.

Out of respect for Clement's father, whom he knew slightly, Monsieur Zabocat invited the young man to dinner. He would have sent Hippolyte to dine in the kitchen with the servants, but Clement and Pauline insisted that he remain. Unhappily, Monsieur Zabocat ordered his servants to set the table for four.

They dined off fine china and silver brought to the island from France. They ate their fill of spicy fish soup, sweet clams, sausage, stuffed land crabs, red beans and rice, rich cakes and fresh fruit.

Monsieur Zabocat was cold but polite during the meal. But when Clement proposed to Pauline and she accepted, he grew furious. "I forbid any such thing. I have decided that we will travel to France," he said. "There you will marry the man *I* choose for you."

But Pauline was a spirited young woman. "No, dear Uncle," she said. "I am of age. And while I thank you for all you have done for me, I must follow my heart."

At this, Monsieur Zabocat swept his dishes off the table. "Then go! None of you is welcome any longer. But have a care," he thundered, his heavy mustache quivering and his dark eyes flashing red, like burning charcoal. "You are not married yet."

Though the hour was late, the three young people set out from Monsieur Zabocat's mansion. The moon hung full as a lamp to light their path. Pauline wept at her uncle's hard-heartedness. Clement comforted his love, assuring her, "My father will welcome you as a daughter when we return to Le Vauclin. And he will make peace with your uncle."

Feeling better, the young woman began to smile. She and Clement talked and laughed together until weariness made all three companions stop to rest. They lay down to sleep under the trees. But the warm night kept Hippolyte awake, and he was troubled to note that the murmur of insects and the sigh of wind in the treetops had died away. In the unnatural silence, he heard the sound of drums — *Tam!* — *Tam!* — *Tamtamtam!* While the others slept, he followed a path that led deeper into the forest.

The drumming led Hippolyte to a small clearing. There he saw three tall, beautiful women whose skin gleamed like polished ebony. One beat upon a small drum. Hippolyte remained hidden when he heard the first woman say, "The pretty girl and the handsome boy are asleep in the grove."

The second said, "Now we must do what the *quimboiseur*, Zabocat, summoned us to do."

"Begin the spell," the third commanded.

At this, Hippolyte grew frightened. He guessed that these creatures were zombies. He prayed they would not discover him before he could learn what wickedness they planned.

The first zombie knelt beside a little stream, cupped water in her hands, and gave some to her companions. "Tomorrow morning," she said, "the couple will come upon a brook."

The second zombie said, "The girl will say that she is thirsty, and the boy will give her water. Then he will take a drink himself."

The third said, "They will die."

Then she cried, "If anyone hears this and repeats this, he will turn into stone from the soles of his feet to his knees."

The zombies slipped away into the shadows while Hippolyte returned to keep watch over his friends.

WHEN THE OTHERS AWOKE at sunrise, Hippolyte dared not tell them what he had seen. He only knew that he must prevent the evil from happening.

Soon the travelers saw a stream, and Pauline asked for a drink. But Hippolyte ran ahead and muddied the water. He brought the young woman some dirty water in his hands, saying, "You would surely fall ill if you took even a drop."

Though all were thirsty, they continued on their way.

WHEN THE SUN was high in the sky, they paused to rest, because the day had grown unbearably hot. While his friends drowsed, leaning against each other in a green shade, Hippolyte anxiously searched the surrounding forest for signs of danger.

Where the trees grew thickest, he spied the three zombies. They were passing a mango one to the other.

"The boy and girl will not escape this time," said the first.

"Soon they will find a mango tree beside the path," said the second.

"They will each eat one and die," said the third. She squeezed the fruit in her hand until juice ran between her fingers. "If anyone hears and tells them what he has heard, he will be turned to stone from the soles of his feet to his chest."

Then the zombies hurried into the forest.

RETURNING, Hippolyte found his friends awake and eager to be on their way. Both said how hungry they felt. Though Hippolyte pointed out the abundance of papayas, cherries, lemons, limes, and bananas all around, Pauline insisted that only a mango would satisfy her, and Clement said the same. Hippolyte dared not tell of what he had heard.

Soon, they came to a huge tree, laden with ripe mangoes. While his companions cried out delightedly, Hippolyte ran ahead. He plucked a fruit, pretended to bite it, then threw it away in disgust.

"Do not taste these!" he cried. "They are poison!" Indeed, his hands were blistered from merely touching the deadly fruit.

Though Clement and Pauline were disappointed, they ignored their hunger, and the three continued on their way.

The nearer they came to home, the hotter the day became. While the others sat and fanned themselves beside the road, Hippolyte restlessly wandered the nearest forest path.

Not far away, he found the zombies passing a serpent from one to the other. "When the pretty couple enters the house," said the first, "their fate is sealed."

"On their wedding night," said the second, "a serpent will sting them to death."

"And if anyone knows and speaks a word," said the third, "he will turn to stone from the soles of his feet to the top of his head." Then she kissed the serpent and led her companions away into the forest.

WHEN THE TRAVELERS reached the plantation, Monsieur Duforce was overjoyed at the news of the engagement of his son to Pauline. He promised to make amends with her uncle.

Indeed, Monsieur Zabocat came for a visit and seemed to forgive the couple; he even agreed to attend their wedding. But Hippolyte saw the poisonous looks behind his pleasant words. He was certain that the man still planned to carry out his vengeance.

By day, Hippolyte was always at his friends' side. At night, he kept watch for the serpent the zombies had threatened, but he saw none. Nevertheless, he knew that the greatest danger awaited Pauline and Clement on their wedding night.

On the day of the wedding, Clement looked more handsome than ever and Pauline was a vision in a white satin gown sewn with diamonds, diamond-studded satin slippers, and a veil of antique French lace that had belonged to Clement's mother. The house and gardens were filled with guests who had come from miles around.

But while the others made merry, Hippolyte sharpened his cutlass. That night, he hid himself in the bridal chamber. As soon as the couple entered the room, Hippolyte saw a long, dark, speckled ribbon glide out from under the bed. It was a *fer de lance*, the deadliest snake on Martinique. With a cry, Hippolyte burst from hiding and cut the serpent in half. Instantly, the pieces vanished.

Clement and Pauline, who had not seen the snake, began to shout at Hippolyte, while Monsieur Duforce and the guests forced open the door. All were astonished to find Hippolyte, cutlass in hand, while no trace of danger remained.

Then Monsieur Zabocat, furious that his plot had failed, cried, "Hippolyte is jealous of his friends' happiness. The sword in his hand is proof that he meant them harm!"

At first, Clement and Pauline and Monsieur Duforce would not believe this. But Hippolyte's refusal to explain his actions angered them. Finally, Clement ordered Hippolyte out of the house. Seeing the coldness in his friend's eyes, Hippolyte desperately began to tell his story. All the while, Monsieur Zabocat accused him, saying, "You are a liar and an assassin!"

When Hippolyte told about the zombies and the poisoned water, he turned to stone up to his knees.

"Say no more!" cried Clement.

Anxious that Clement know the whole truth, Hippolyte explained about the deadly fruit. So he became stone up to his chest.

"Not another word," begged Pauline, clutching his hand. She shivered at the feel of hard, cold stone.

Finally, Hippolyte told about the serpent. Instantly, he turned to stone to the very top of his head.

"Oh, my poor friend!" shouted Clement. "I would give anything to restore you to life!"

Suddenly, an old man stepped from the crowd.

"I can bring back his life," he said to Clement, "if you will take this curse upon yourself."

"Yes," Clement answered. "I already owe him my life three times over." Then he bravely hugged Pauline.

The old man passed his hand three times over the head of the statue, then blew gently into the stone face.

Hippolyte became a living person once more. Then the stranger turned toward Clement as Pauline and the others looked on in horror. But Monsieur Zabocat leaned forward eagerly.

The old man made as if to touch Clement, but instead his outstretched finger suddenly touched Monsieur Zabocat's forehead. The man instantly became a stone figure.

"Your willingness to sacrifice your life for your friend gave me the power to break the spell," the stranger said to Clement, "but a curse only ends when returned to its source."

While the friends exchanged a heartfelt embrace, the old man said, "I was the beggar you gave a Christian burial to on your way to Macouba. *Bon-Die*, the good Lord, gave me permission to come to earth and do you this service in return."

The next moment, he vanished.

AFTER THIS, Clement and Pauline lived happily together. Hippolyte fell in love and married, too, and the children of both couples grew up as close as brothers and sisters.

The statue that had been Monsieur Zabocat was placed in a corner of the garden, where it soon crumbled into dust.

THIS NARRATIVE is based on a story from the island of Martinique in the French West Indies recorded in Elsie Clews Parsons's *Folk-Lore of the Antilles, French and English*, published by the American Folk-Lore Society in 1943. I have consulted variants from the Cape Verde Islands, the Dominican Republic, Argentina, Chile, Puerto Rico, and Brazil.

The root story can be traced back to European sources—most notably, "Faithful John" or "Faithful Joannes" by the brothers Grimm, which provided details for my retelling. For a fuller list of variants, see *The Types of the Folk-Tale* by Antti Arne, translated and enlarged by Stith Thompson in 1928—specifically, tale type 516. In the most familiar version of this tale, the faithful servant helps his master (who has fallen in love with a painting of a distant princess) carry his beloved across the sea from her father—only to fall victim to the curses of a trio of ravens that lands on the boat as it sails homeward.

The Martiniquan version appealed to me because of its unique setting and incorporation of tale type 505 (the grateful dead/the dead man as helper) and tale type 506 (the rescued princess/the grateful dead man). The return of the ghost provides for the faithful servant's rescue without resorting to the more common motif of slaying the couple's firstborn child (who will be magically restored to life) so that the child's blood can bring life back to the statue.

This version also appealed because of its identification of the three "voices in the night" as zombies (a distinctly West Indian wrinkle) and—especially—its emphasis on the friendship of black and white characters.

The wicked guardian is drawn from parallels outside Martinique in which a father, father-in-law, or step-mother curses the errant child. Such a character seems necessary to explain the sudden appearance of evil creatures with a particular malice directed at the eloping couple.

—R.S.S.